MO'S MISCHIEF

Four Troublemakers

Other titles in the Mo's Mischief series:

MO'S MISCHIEF

Four Troublemakers

Hongying Yang

HarperCollins *Children's Books*

First published in China by Jieli Publishing House 2003
First published in Great Britain by HarperCollins *Children's Books* 2008
HarperCollins *Children's Books* is a division of HarperCollins*Publishers* Ltd
77-85 Fulham Palace Road, Hammersmith, London W6 8JB

The HarperCollins *Children's Books* website address is
www.harpercollinschildrensbooks.co.uk

1

ISBN-13 978-0-00-727339-3
ISBN-10 0-00-727339-8

Printed and bound in England by
Clays Ltd, St Ives plc

MO'S TROUBLES

Mo Shen Ma had a problem. It was a new kind of problem – one he'd never come across before. It wasn't a problem caused by his mischievous ways, or a problem with his Maths homework. It wasn't even a problem with Man-Man, his desk-mate who wrote in her notebook every time Mo did anything wrong. No, this was a problem called... *jealousy*!

It all began on school Sports' Day. This was always held at a stadium just outside the city. The children had all been given a packed lunch from school which included a hard boiled egg, a bun and a bottle of milk.

Da – known as Hippo because he had a mouth as big as a hippo's – took his boiled egg from his lunchbox and cracked it open on his forehead.

All the girls thought Hippo was the coolest guy in class, not just because he was tall and tough, but because he didn't talk much – he was the strong, silent type.

Lily treated Hippo differently from the other boys.

Lily was the prettiest girl in the class and was as proud as a princess. She didn't talk much to boys, especially boys who always got into trouble, like Mo. But Hippo never tried to talk to the girls, and that made Lily curious. Because Hippo never tried to talk to her, she grabbed every opportunity to talk to him!

"Hippo, did your forehead hurt when you cracked that egg?"

"Not at all," said Hippo, putting the egg in his mouth and swallowing it in one big gulp.

This wasn't such an extraordinary thing for someone with a big mouth to do. But to Lily, who was very lady-like and always ate in dainty little bites, eating an egg in one bite was AMAZING.

Lily stood next to Hippo waiting to ask him to do her a favour. But before she'd had a chance to open her mouth, some other girls pushed her aside and said to Hippo, "Why did you crack open the egg using your forehead?"

"No reason," said Hippo.

"Wow! That's so cool!" the girls screamed.

The girls all gave their boiled eggs to Hippo.

Crack! Crack! Crack!

Hippo cracked more than twenty eggs, one by one,

on his forehead. Even some of the boys joined in and gave their eggs to Hippo.

Hippo noticed that Mo was staring at him angrily. He thought perhaps Mo wanted his egg cracked open. But when Hippo offered, Mo said he could crack his own egg, thank you very much. He wasn't impressed with Hippo's trick. Anyone could crack eggshells on their foreheads.

Mo closed his eyes and tried cracking his egg on his forehead.

"Ouch!"

It hurt so much that Mo jumped up, clutching his forehead. But the egg wasn't even cracked!

"Mo, do it harder!" said Hippo.

Mo held the egg further away from his forehead. But when he was just about to crack it really hard, he chickened out.

"Mo, do it!" said Hippo, encouragingly.

"What if I break my head?" Mo moaned.

Hippo called Mo a chicken.

The girls all started laughing at Mo.

Those girls are all out of their minds! thought Mo. *How can girls as smart as Man-Man and as pretty as Lily fall for a big-mouth like Hippo?*

Mo noticed that Lily was sidling up to Hippo again. Hippo blushed and couldn't even look Lily in the eye. Mo wandered closer, pretending not to pay any attention to them. He wanted to find out what the two of them were up to.

"Hippo, will you crack open an egg for me?" asked Lily.

"No problem."

As soon as Lily handed over her egg, Hippo cracked it open on his forehead and gave it back to Lily.

"Hippo, could you do me another favour?"

"With pleasure."

"Could you eat my egg?"

"Of course."

Mo saw Hippo shove the whole egg into his mouth and swallow it in one big gulp.

Mo was getting more and more upset with Hippo's showing off. Then he saw Lily sharing her drink with him.

Mo was jealous because Lily had never been that nice to *him*. Mo had never felt like jealous before, and he didn't like it one little bit.

But things were about to get even worse.

One of the highlights of Sports' Day was the year group football matches. And the Year 4 Football Match was scheduled to take place in the afternoon.

Hippo was goalie and he was BRILLIANT. His mouth may have been big, but he made the goal mouth seem really small! He headed every ball away, time and time again.

Hippo's performance was amazing. After every save, he celebrated like a Premier League player, running around the pitch, hugging everyone he ran into, even kneeling on the ground and kissing the grass.

After the game was over, Hippo was the centre of attention. He was surrounded by girls. Some handed him bottles of water, others gave him tissues to wipe the sweat from his face. Lily even bent down and tied up Hippo's shoelaces for him.

Mo had had enough of this. He normally hated anyone telling tales to the teacher – mainly because he was fed up with people telling tales on him – but jealousy had made him blind.

"Ms Qin, I have something to tell you."

"Mo, what's the matter with you?" Ms Qin noticed

Mo wasn't being his normal self.

"Hippo ate Lily's egg for lunch today."

"Why did he do that? Didn't he have one of his own?"

"Lily gave it to him."

"Is that all you wanted to say, Mo?" Ms Qin smiled. "I thought you had something more important to tell me."

Ms Qin thought Mo was acting very strangely today. She knew he was a bit of a scamp, and very naughty, but he was really a kind-hearted and generous boy. He didn't usually worry about petty things like someone giving someone else their lunch to eat.

"Ms Qin, didn't you tell us this afternoon that we shouldn't waste food?"

"But who exactly was it that wasted food?"

"Lily did, because she gave her egg to Hippo."

"Maybe Lily gave the egg to Hippo to give him energy for the match. I think that's a nice thing to do! And he did play very well…"

Mo stared. Surely Hippo's performance in goal hadn't had anything to do with eating Lily's egg?

"But Ms Qin …"

Ms Qin was growing impatient with Mo and cut him off. "Mo, just what is *wrong* with you today?"

Mo knew exactly what was wrong with him. He was jealous. And he hated it.

MO GETS MAD

Lily was the prettiest girl in Mo's class. She always tilted her chin upwards when she walked and never took any notice of the boys in class, Mo included. But suddenly she was being really nice to Hippo. Why had she singled out Hippo for attention and not Mo? Was it really just because Hippo could crack eggshells on his forehead?

But Mo wanted Lily to take notice of *him*, Mo Shen Ma! Then he had an idea! He decided that if *he* could break eggshells on his forehead, maybe Lily would start to treat him the way she treated Hippo – just maybe.

Mo started practising cracking eggs on his forehead. He found out it was quite easy. He couldn't do it before because he was afraid it would hurt. The trick was to shut your eyes and not think about whether it was going to hurt or not. With a quick knock of the egg on the forehead, the eggshells would crack. Mo's forehead did hurt a *little* bit, but it wasn't too bad.

After Mo had learned how to crack eggs on his forehead, he practised eating boiled eggs whole. Mo didn't really like hardboiled eggs, because of their smell, but he decided that he had to learn to like them if he was going to impress Lily.

So, after he'd mastered the forehead egg-cracking trick, he started to take hard-boiled eggs to school every day for his lunch.

Mo's desk-mate, Man-Man, was Lily's best friend. During break, Lily always went over to Man-Man's desk for a chat. Whenever Lily came over, Mo tried to hang around. But Man-Man and Lily wanted Mo to leave them alone.

"Mo, why don't you go out to the playground with the other boys?"

"I don't feel like going out."

Mo took out the egg he'd brought from home and quickly cracked it open on his forehead. He thought that Man-Man and Lily would scream in amazement at what he'd done, but they didn't.

Man-Man took out her little notebook – the one she used to note down Mo's mischievous behaviour in class. Man-Man wrote down that Mo had brought food into class. Mo couldn't have cared less what she wrote in the notebook, he had grown so used to it. The worst that could happen was that he would be called into Ms Qin's office to be told off.

Lily stared at Mo as if he was an idiot.

Mo couldn't swallow the egg whole like Hippo, because his mouth was nowhere near as big as Hippo's. It took Mo at least four bites to finish his egg.

Mo stretched his neck, eyes bulging, and struggled to finish the last bite of the egg. Then he told Lily, "I can help you finish your egg, if you like," he said.

"What makes you think I've got an egg?" replied Lily, irritably.

This wasn't going very well.

"I mean… if you don't like eating eggs, I could eat them for you," Mo grovelled.

"Even if I had an egg, I wouldn't give it to *you*!" Lily yelled.

Lily turned around to leave. Her hair was tied back into a long ponytail. As she turned, her ponytail slapped Mo right in the face.

Every day, the four troublemakers – Mo, Hippo, Monkey and Penguin – would walk home together from school. The four of them didn't live very near each other, but they always took the same way home so that they could plan a little mischief together.

On this particular day, Monkey had one arm over Hippo's shoulder and the other over Mo's shoulder and he said, "Hey, my older cousin's class is having a Miss 6-1 Contest."

"What's a Miss 6-1 Contest?" asked Mo.

"You guys don't know what a Miss 6-1 is?" Monkey looked smug. "Miss 6-1 is the prettiest girl in the 1st class of Year Six. So, Miss City Primary would be …"

"The prettiest girl in the whole school!" Penguin blurted out.

"Hey, why don't we nominate a girl to be Miss 4-1?" 4-1 was the first class of Year 4 – Mo's class!

Hippo nominated Lily, but Mo disagreed.

"I'm not nominating Lily."

"Who are you going to nominate then?"

Mo thought Lily *was* the prettiest girl in class, but he didn't want to nominate her because he was still angry about the way she'd been so nice to Hippo.

"I know who Mo's going to nominate," Monkey said.

"Who?"

"He's going to nominate Angel!"

Monkey quickly made a run for it before Mo could hit him. The other boys were always teasing Mo about Angel. She was his neighbour and he played with her a lot after school. The other boys were always saying that Mo fancied her, but to Mo she was just the girl next door.

Mo wasn't going to let Monkey get away with it and started to run after him. But Hippo stopped him and asked him, "Why won't you nominate Lily to be Miss 4-1?"

"I just *won't*," Mo said, crossly.

Mo had a series of flashbacks. He remembered Lily

17

kneeling down and tying up Hippo's shoelaces; he thought of Lily giving her egg to Hippo. Mo also remembered the way Lily had stared at him when *he* cracked an egg on his forehead, as if he was an idiot; and he remembered how Lily's ponytail had slapped him in the face...

"She's mean, she's ugly, and she's a dinosaur!"

A dinosaur – that was just about the biggest insult Mo could think of.

Hippo grabbed Mo by the collar. "Take that back... or I'll... I'll....!"

Mo wasn't about to back down.

"I won't take it back! In fact, I'll say it again! Lily is a *dinosaur*!"

Hippo shoved Mo. Mo shoved Hippo. Then Hippo went to shove Mo again, but Mo jumped out of the way. Hippo ended up shoving Penguin instead. Penguin was eating a chocolate bar but when Hippo pushed him the chocolate fell out of his hand... on to the pavement where a passing dog quickly ate it! Mo couldn't help laughing... and neither could Penguin or Hippo. OK, they'd had an argument, but what had it been about? A girl and a stupid beauty contest! Friends were MUCH more important!

MONKEY RABBITS ON

No one talked more rubbish than Monkey. He never stopped talking and he never kept still. He was always gibbering on about something or other, leaping around all over the place. That was why everyone called him Monkey, even though his real name was Chao. Nine out of ten things he said were pure nonsense.

Monkey's parents were fed up of being called into school because their son talked so much rubbish. They couldn't understand why he did it, and who he'd got it from. Neither his mother nor his father *ever* talked nonsense.

So, just where did Monkey get his habit of talking rubbish from?

Monkey's father thought very hard and finally remembered something from before Monkey was born. He asked Monkey's mother, "When you were pregnant, didn't you love eating rabbit?"

"Yes, that's right," Monkey's mother said. "When I was pregnant with Monkey, I craved rabbit stew. And I ate it every day until Monkey was born!"

"Ah-ha!" Monkey's father thought he'd finally cracked it. "You ate too much rabbit stew when you were pregnant, that's why our boy rabbits on all the time!"

Monkey's nonsense-talking usually started in the morning as soon as he woke up.

Every morning when Monkey got out of bed, he would put on his slippers and have a good stretch. Then he strolled on to the balcony where his mother would be watering the flowers. Monkey knew that his mother wouldn't listen to his nonsense, so instead, he would talk to the flowers.

"A little sunshine and moonshine to make you grow; too much water and showers and you will wither and mould," he rabbited on.

"For goodness sake, Monkey, stop talking nonsense! Go inside and eat your breakfast or you'll be late for school!" Monkey's mother would yell.

"It's your fault for eating too much rabbit stew," Monkey mumbled while finishing his breakfast.

Monkey went off to school.

A teenage boy with dyed blond hair came towards him. Seeing the teenage boy, Monkey started mumbling:

"You think you're so cool, you think you're so smart, but your hair's a mess, and your clothes are too dark. That belt you're wearing is way out of date. You think you're the best, but what about the rest?"

"You talkin' about me, kid?" Blondie challenged Monkey.

"Nope, not *you*," Monkey replied.

"Then who were you talkin' about?"

"Him!"

Monkey pointed behind Blondie's shoulder, and as Blondie turned to look, Monkey ran off.

Monkey bumped into Hippo on his way to school.

"Hippo, let me tell you a story: a long time ago, there was a fool. No matter what question he was being asked, his only answer was 'no'. Have you heard that story, Hippo?"

"No," said Hippo not in the mood for Monkey's rabbiting.

"Ha, fooled you! You said NO! That makes you the fool!" Monkey laughed as he ran off.

Hippo chased after Monkey, wanting to teach him a lesson. Monkey pleaded for mercy and told him he had another story, a much better one.

"A long time ago, there was a hunter. One day, the hunter saw a pig. So the hunter shot the pig with his rifle. Just as the hunter was walking towards the pig, the pig suddenly rolled over. Do you know why?"

Hippo thought hard.

"The pig was wondering why, too!"

Hippo groaned. Monkey had fooled him again.

When Monkey got to the classroom, he heard Wen boasting about something to the girls. The girls seemed enchanted by Wen's story.

Monkey picked up his pencil case and started knocking it on his desk, making a rhythm to accompany a new little song:

"*Why does the chicken go home to roost?*

Cos somebody's making a mighty big boast!"

Monkey had caught the girls' attention.

"Monkey, are you saying that Wen was boasting?"

"I was *not* boasting. I was telling the truth," said Wen.

Just then the bell rang.

When the class ended, Lily happened to walk by Monkey's seat. Monkey began rapping again while he accompanied himself with his pencil case.

"Lily, Lily, turning her head, a croc in the river was shocked to death; Lily, Lily, turning her head, all the boys went mighty red. Lily, Lily, turning her head..."

Mo, who sat behind Monkey, laughed so hard that he started hiccupping.

"Stop laughing!" Man-Man yelled at Mo, before turning to Monkey.

"Monkey, stop bullying Lily!" she yelled.

"I wasn't bulling," said Monkey. "I was simply praising Lily's beauty."

"You are a toad yearning after a swan," Mo said to Monkey.

Lily was a ballet dancer and was so good that she

had already been in a performance of *Swan Lake* on TV. Mo was comparing Lily to the swan and Monkey to the toad.

"*A soldier who does not dream of becoming general is not a good soldier; Likewise, a toad that does not yearn after a swan is not a good toad.*"

When Lily heard this nonsense from Monkey, she burst out laughing.

But Man-Man got even angrier. She was angry with Monkey, angry with Mo, and even angry with Lily.

Monkey saw Man-Man staring at the three of them with her big round eyes, and a new piece of nonsense came out of his mouth:

"*Your eyes are like twinkling stars in the sky, bright and clear and shiny;*

Your eyes are like the autumn moon – it's a pity your brain is tiny."

Man-Man stood up and ran out of the classroom.

"She's going to tell Ms Qin what you said." Mo was beginning to enjoy the whole thing. It was nice to see someone else in trouble for a change.

As expected, Ms Qin asked Monkey to stay for detention after school.

"Monkey, why do you always talk so much nonsense?"

Ms Qin couldn't even remember how many times she'd asked Monkey the same question.

"It is all my mum's fault. She ate too much rabbit stew when she was having me—"

"All right, enough of the rabbit stew story!"

Ms Qin couldn't remember how many times she's heard the "rabbit stew" excuse.

"When will you stop talking such nonsense and start behaving sensibly?"

"I shall stop it right away," Monkey said sincerely.

Ms Qin let Monkey go home. She felt he had learned his lesson at last.

But on his way back home, Monkey saw Blondie, the teenage boy, breakdancing in the street. He was wearing a baseball cap, had headphones plugged in his ears, and had his iPod clipped to his jeans' pocket.

This was just too tempting and Monkey couldn't help himself.

"You think you're so cool,
But you drink in the pool,
And your mouth is full of drool.
You think you're the best,
But you're just a pest. You're—"

The boy made one leaping dance move and landed right next to Monkey. Then he kicked Monkey in the backside.

Now Monkey really had learned his lesson!

PENGUIN'S FART

Penguin was short, chubby, and always wore black cowboy shirts. He never bothered to do up his buttons properly, and never seemed to mind showing his fat, round tummy. And because he was chubby, he waddled when he walked, just like a penguin. That's how he got his nickname – Penguin – even though he was really called Fei.

But Penguin was known for something else too – his farts. Whenever he giggled suddenly in class, you knew he'd just done a silent but deadly one. Not that Penguin's farts were always silent. He made all kinds of noises when he farted: sometimes it was like a machine-gun being fired; sometimes like a single cannonball shot into the air; sometimes the sound was rhythmic like a saxophone, and sometimes it dragged on like Chinese string instruments.

But most often, it was a sound like tearing cloth.

Once, during Maths class, the Maths teacher had just got to the most important part of the lesson. He turned towards the blackboard to write down some notes for the children. The classroom was very quiet, except for the sound of chalk on the blackboard. Suddenly, there was the sound of cloth being torn.

"Who's making that sound?"

The Maths teacher was very strict. He couldn't stand children who talked or messed around in his class.

The children stared at each other, not sure where the sound had come from or what it was.

"Who was ripping something up?" The Maths teacher asked one more time.

Mo turned round and asked Penguin, "Was it you?"

The Maths teacher stepped away from his desk.

"It *wasn't* me."

Penguin acted as if he hadn't done anything wrong.

"I wasn't doing anything, and I wasn't ripping anything up either."

It wasn't really Penguin's fault, because farting is just a way of expelling gas from the body – it's natural!

But Penguin had a problem: he always had to fart standing up. Mo was the first person to find out about this. It was on a day when he and Penguin were on their bikes. They were cycling uphill, and both boys were pedalling as hard as they could. Just as they were about to reach the top of the hill, Penguin suddenly stood up on his pedals.

"Penguin, why aren't you pedalling?"

"I need to fart!"

Penguin's bike went backwards down the hill, and Penguin fell off. The unpleasant accident left Penguin with a bruised and swollen bum cheek.

It was Ms Qin who helped Penguin get rid of the annoying habit of farting in the classroom.

During a Chinese lesson, Ms Qin and the rest of the class were reading from the textbook when Penguin suddenly stood up and then quickly sat back down again.

"Penguin, what were you doing?"

"I was just expelling gas, Ms Qin."

"Why did you have to stand up then?"

"I can't do it sitting down."

The whole class laughed very hard, and no one could focus on their lesson for the rest of the morning.

Ms Qin was cross. Whenever Ms Qin got cross, her face went very red and her voice got very shrill. Ms Qin asked Penguin to write 100 lines in his exercise book: "I must not expel gas in class".

But Penguin refused. He hadn't done anything wrong. If his body wanted to get rid of gas, it must be allowed to do so. It was natural.

"Why are you refusing to write the lines, Penguin?"

"Because I didn't do anything wrong, Ms Qin."

"But you did, Penguin. You broke a classroom rule – you expelled gas in class, and you stood up," said Ms Qin, smiling.

"I didn't do it on purpose."

Penguin started sobbing. He had always been a bit of a cry-baby.

Ms Qin softened a bit when she saw Penguin's tears. "We'll forget about it this time," she said, "as long as you stop expelling gas in class. All right?"

"I didn't mean to, but I can't help it," said Penguin.

Ms Qin held Penguin's chubby hands very softly and said, "Penguin, I trust you. I'm sure you can control your gas."

Penguin was so touched that he was determined not to fart in class again, for Ms Qin's sake.

And for the next few days, Mo didn't hear the sound of Penguin's farts. He wondered how Penguin was managing this time.

"Penguin, what's happened to all your farts?"

Penguin pointed to his fat tummy. "They're all in here."

"If your tummy is full of gas, do you think you can float like a balloon?" Mo imagined a chubby penguin floating in the sky.

Penguin was acting mysteriously. He looked around and signalled for Mo to come closer.

When Mo was standing next to him, Penguin whispered, "I'm only going to tell this to you, so don't tell anyone else."

After Mo agreed to keep the secret, Penguin finally said in a low murmur, "I have floated before."

"Are you serious?" Mo's jaw dropped to the floor. "Hurry up and tell me!"

"Do you know how I stopped farting?"

This was exactly what Mo wanted to find out.

Penguin went on: "I was saving all of the gas in my tummy. When there was enough gas, my feet left the ground and I floated like a balloon. I floated higher and higher, higher than the tree tops, higher than houses and higher than TV towers …I even saw an aeroplane flying above me. I was planning on floating higher than the aeroplane, but I remembered Mum was cooking sweet and sour pork-ribs for dinner, so I came down."

"How did you get down?"

"When all the gas in a balloon escapes, what happens to the balloon?" Penguin asked Mo in return.

"The balloon comes down."

"Yes, very good." Penguin patted Mo on the head: "So then I started expelling the gas from my tummy little by little, in little farts, and I came down little by little. *Parp, Parp, Parp! Parp, Parp, Parp!!* When I had farted all the gas out, I was back on the ground."

Mo stared at Penguin, speechless.

"Mo, you must be jealous of me, because I can save gas in my tummy and float in the air," said Penguin.

"What, do you think I'm that stupid?!" Mo shouted.

"But you *were* stupid enough to listen to my story!!"

Penguin was determined never to tell anyone what really made him stop farting in class. He didn't want anyone thinking *he* was the teacher's pet...

CHEWING STEEL

Penguin's little problem was all to do with his eating. Penguin loved eating more than anything, and he loved taking food to school. His shirt and trouser pockets were always full of different kinds of snacks: there were various kinds of chocolate, chicken-flavoured crisps, beef jerky and butter-cream rice crackers. Penguin was like a walking snack shop.

Penguin ate all day long, even in the classroom – which was strictly against the rules. He was expert at eating snacks in secret. The best time to eat snacks was when the teacher was writing something on the blackboard. But there were other opportunities as well. When the teacher was reading from the textbook, Penguin would lower his head and pretend to read from his textbook too; but in fact, he was secretly putting a snack into his mouth. Even when the teacher was facing the class, Penguin had a way of putting food into his mouth right under the teacher's nose. He would pretend to drop his pencil on the floor, then he'd quickly shove food into his mouth as he bent down to pick it up.

If the teacher ever blinked, Penguin would put a snack into his mouth at lightning speed, and then pretend to nod at the teacher, fooling the teacher into thinking that he was paying attention to the lesson.

Penguin's desk-mate, Lily, knew that Penguin ate during lessons, but she never asked for food. Lily was a ballet dancer and was very careful not to eat the sort of fattening food Penguin brought to class.

At break time, Penguin would eat his least favourite snacks – things like cheap sweets and very dry beef jerky. This was because he knew that whenever they saw their friend's jaw moving, Mo,

Hippo and Monkey would come over and demand snacks. If Penguin refused to share, they would tickle him until he dropped them!

But there was one snack Penguin knew he could eat anywhere and at anytime. Penguin's auntie had brought this snack back from Japan. Penguin ate it during lessons *and* at playtime. He knew that none of his friends would want to try it, or try to take it from him, because no one else would *dare* to eat it.

"Penguin, what are you eating?"

"Steel balls."

"How can you eat steel balls?!"

Mo and the rest of the boys couldn't believe their eyes.

Penguin took out a handful of steel balls from his trousers' pocket: "Guys, take a good look, tell me what you see."

Those really were steel balls! They were pea-sized and made of metal that shone in Penguin's palm.

Penguin threw a couple of steel balls into his mouth and chewed them, making a loud chewing noise as if it was the most natural thing to chew. He even dared Hippo to try a couple.

Although Hippo had a big mouth and could swallow eggs whole, he wasn't going to eat steel balls – he didn't want to break his teeth.

Then Penguin asked Monkey whether *he* wanted to try them.

But that was out of the question for Monkey, because he'd worn a brace for a year and wasn't going to have more metal in his mouth – especially not steel balls.

Finally Penguin asked Mo whether he wanted to try them

"What do they taste like?" Mo asked.

"Duh – steel balls taste like steel balls!" Penguin said.

Mo had another question, "But why do you want to eat steel balls in the first place?"

"What do you mean 'why'?" Penguin was getting fed up with this interrogation. "I wanted to eat them so that I can show you how tough my teeth are!"

Penguin opened his mouth and showed them his teeth, all of them crooked and some a little cracked.

Mo was amazed. Now he had two friends who could do incredible things. One who could crack eggshells on his forehead, and another who could eat steel balls!

Even Hippo and Monkey stopped thinking of Penguin as a nobody. Penguin had always been their little sidekick in the Gang of Four. The other three boys used to order him around: when they played football, Penguin held all of their book bags; when they had water-gun fights, Penguin looked after their clothes; on the school picnic, Penguin was the one who had to fan the fire. But now they knew that Penguin could chew steel balls, they didn't feel like they could boss him around anymore. If they bossed Penguin around, he might throw a few steel balls into his mouth and chew them loudly. Then he might stare at the boys fiercely and say: "You can only boss me around if you dare to chew steel balls!"

But none of the boys dared to chew steel balls, so they had no choice but to be nicer to Penguin…

If Penguin hadn't leaked the secret of the steel balls to Lily, Mo and the other boys might never have bossed him around again.

Penguin's desk-mate was Lily — the prettiest girl in class. Penguin knew that Lily had been impressed that Hippo could crack eggshells on his forehead. So he said to Lily, " So what? Hippo might be able to crack eggs on his forehead, but did you know that some people can chew steel balls?"

"Who could possibly chew steel balls?" Lily asked.

"The person who could chew steel balls is closer than you think…"

"Who is it? If you don't tell me, I won't believe you."

"It's me, it's me!" Penguin said.

"You?"

"Take a look at these." Penguin took a couple of steel balls from his pocket.

Lily inspected them closely and confirmed that they were really steel balls.

Penguin threw them into his mouth and chewed loudly.

"Aaaahh!" Lily screamed.

Penguin was pleased by her shocked reaction.

But Penguin was a bit too pleased with himself and it made him careless. After he'd swallowed the steel balls, he opened up his mouth for Lily to inspect. As she looked, Lily thought she could smell something fruity.

Why do those steel balls smell fruity? she thought.

"Let me have another look at those steel balls," Lily said.

Penguin handed over a steel ball.

Lily looked very carefully at the steel ball. It looked real enough. When Penguin wasn't paying attention, Lily quickly put the steel ball in her mouth. At first, it tasted quite cool, but then Lily thought it started tasting sweet. Little by little, there was a taste of fruit, and the taste was getting stronger and stronger. Lily chewed on it and crushed the steel ball, and suddenly, her mouth was filled with the taste of fruit.

The steel balls were sweets!

Very soon, Mo, Hippo and Monkey all knew the secret of the steel balls. The three boys searched Penguin's book bag and found a beautifully made glass container filled with steel ball sweets. The container had Japanese characters written on it that said "Steel Fruit Drops".

Mo, Hippo and Monkey scoffed all the steel fruit drops that were left in the glass container, making the loudest chewing noises they could. They'd show Penguin that he could never out-trick them again!

WHO'LL BE BOSS?

One day after school, just as Mo, Hippo, Monkey and Penguin walked out of the main school gate, they caught sight of a super-long car parked outside. Monkey said he'd seen cars like that on TV. They were for really important people, like presidents or pop stars.

But Penguin said the vehicle was called an RV, and it belonged to his dad.

None of the boys had ever heard of an RV before.

"You guys don't know what an RV is? An RV is a Recreational Vehicle. It's like a house on wheels,"

Penguin explained. "You can do lots of things in an RV, like hold meetings, go on holiday, sleep, drink, have friends over ... anyway, I have to run now, because dad's come to pick me up."

There was no question of the man in the RV being anyone but Penguin's father, because just like Penguin, he was also chubby with a fat tummy. If Penguin was like a baby penguin, then his father was like a big penguin. His father was wearing a dinner jacket, white shirt and a black bow tie. He looked even more like a penguin than Penguin!

Penguin got into the huge RV, and his dad drove away in a hurry. The boys – Mo, Hippo and Monkey, were dumbfounded. Hippo's huge mouth stayed open for ages.

"I didn't know Penguin's parents were so rich!" Mo said.

Hippo said, "Yeah, but even though Penguin is rich, he's very stingy."

That was true. Penguin was the stingiest of the four boys. He never liked sharing anything with his friends and he always moaned that he never had any pocket money left. Sometimes, the four boys would get takeaways from KFC or McDonalds. Everyone agreed to share the bill, but Penguin sometimes said he didn't have any money, or couldn't put in as much as the others. And he always ate the most!

The next day after school, the four boys went home together as usual. Penguin asked the others, "Do you guys know where I went yesterday?"

Who cared where he went?

"Do you want to know? I went to a BANQUET."

The boys knew about parties and balls, but not banquets.

"A banquet a very posh meal."

"Why were you at the banquet?" the boys wanted to know.

"I had to be there because everyone in my father's company was there. In the future, I will be their boss, so I went there to meet with my future employees!"

"Wow, you're going to be the boss of your father's company?!"

The boys were impressed.

"In the future, when I'm the boss, if you guys are still my best buddies, I will promote you all," Penguin boasted.

Penguin patted Mo, Hippo and Monkey on their shoulders, acting as if he was already the boss.

Mo shoved Hippo and Monkey aside and said, "When you become the boss of your dad's company, what can I be?"

"You can be the General Manager!"

"But if I'm the General Manager, what will you be?" Mo thought the General Manager was the most senior person in a company.

"I will be the CEO of course! The Chief Executive Officer!"

"Does the CEO boss the General Manager around? Or is it the other way around?"

Penguin was getting impatient. "The CEO is the biggest boss, and the General Manager is the second biggest boss."

Then Monkey and Hippo began nagging Penguin.

"But Penguin, I want to be the General Manager too!"

"Penguin, me too, me too!"

Mo shoved Hippo aside and said: "Your mouth is too big. You can't be General Manager. Besides, Penguin has already promised *me* the position of General Manager, right Penguin?"

But Penguin was thinking about food. He said to the boys, "Well, you'll have to compete for the title, you guys."

Penguin walked away and started to eat some cream-filled rice crackers. No one was forcing him to share his food right now, since the other boys all wanted to compete to become the General Manager.

To Hippo and Mo, competing meant only one thing: wrestling! The two boys soon began wrestling. Hippo liked to trip up his rivals, and Mo soon tripped over Hippo's feet and fell to the ground.

Penguin was enjoying watching Mo and Hippo rolling on the ground. He was also enjoying his snacks.

But Mo wasn't as strong as Hippo. He was getting tired of wrestling and decided to give in. "All right, all right, I give in. You can be the General Manager."

Hippo rolled around and stood up, and then he helped Mo up from the ground and told Penguin loudly, "Penguin, I won!"

"Sure, sure," Penguin replied half-heartedly. "You can be the General Manager then!"

"But what about me?" Mo said.

Penguin was still eating rice crackers and answered, "OK, you can be the Manager then."

But Monkey suddenly said: "Let me, let me! I want to be the Manager!"

Penguin waved to the two boys: "You can compete for it, boys!"

So Mo had to wrestle again, this time with Monkey.

Monkey liked to lock his opponent in place with his arms. As soon as the wrestling match began, Monkey leaped towards Mo and pinned him with his arms. The two boys were intertwined like two snakes.

Once again, Penguin enjoyed watching the wrestling match while eating his snacks.

But Mo and Monkey remained locked together for so long that Penguin got bored. He'd already finished a whole bag of rice crackers. Penguin asked whether Hippo wanted to leave and go home.

Since Hippo had already been appointed General Manager, he couldn't care less who won the match, so he and Penguin left.

Mo and Monkey were still in an arm lock long after Penguin and Hippo had left. It was Monkey who first realised the other two boys had gone.

"Mo, Penguin's left already. So he can't say which one of us is Manager!"

"Well, get up then and let go of me, quickly!" Mo said.

But Monkey wouldn't let go of Mo. He said he would only let go if Mo let him be the Manager.

"All right! All right! You can be the Manager! What do I care?"

After two lost matches, Mo suddenly felt the whole thing was very stupid.

Now that Monkey had won the job of Manager, he began to feel sorry for Mo. He promised to talk to Penguin the next day and see if he would let Mo be Monkey's personal bodyguard.

The following day, as promised, Monkey asked Penguin if he would let Mo be his bodyguard.

 49

"Bodyguard? What are you talking about?" Penguin had already forgotten about their little game from yesterday.

But Hippo hadn't forgotten. "Penguin, you promised to let me be the General Manager when you take over your father's company. I wrestled Mo for it. And Monkey is going to be the Manager, because he beat Mo as well."

"Oh, yes," said Penguin. "Of course." He looked at Mo. "But why would I want you to be my bodyguard? You lost both your wrestling matches. You'd be a hopeless bodyguard! Let me think... ah, that's it! You can be my secretary!"

TEAMWORK

Penguin was always showing off to his classmates about his father and his father's four brothers who worked in different parts of the world – one on each continent. Penguin's father was the oldest of the five, and worked in China; the second youngest worked in Germany; the third youngest worked in the United States; the fourth youngest worked in Brazil; and the youngest worked in Australia.

With so many of his relatives living abroad, Penguin thought he knew a lot about the world.

Mo had heard about lots of things from Penguin:

RVs, hamburgers and pizzas, snowboarding and surfing, cowboys and even cowgirls! Mo forgot most of what he heard from Penguin since he was not that interested in Penguin's showing off. But there was one thing Penguin told him that Mo remembered very well: children in primary schools in other countries are dismissed very early in the afternoon – around three in the afternoon. When they get home, they can do *anything* they want: they can watch TV, play computer games, listen to their iPods or phone their friends on their mobiles.

Children at Mo's primary school weren't dismissed until four-thirty in the afternoon – one and a half hours later than children in other parts of the world! On top of that, children in China weren't allowed to go home after lessons were over; instead, they had to stay in school for the After School Homework Session from four-thirty till five-thirty. At the After School Homework Session, children were chosen to be in charge of the entire class, to make sure that everyone finished their homework for the day: first, Maths homework, and then Chinese homework. And when there was nothing else to do, if the After School Homework Session wasn't officially over, the children's minds would wander. They'd start thinking about all sorts of strange things...

On one particular day, during the After School Homework Session, Mo was thinking about a slice of cake decorated with a cherry on top. The cream in the cake was pale and golden, and the cherry was as crimson as a holly berry. Mo wondered whether he should eat the cake first and then eat the cherry, or the cherry first and then the cake?

It was a *very* difficult question. Mo turned to ask his desk-mate, Man-Man. "Hey Man-Man, if you had a slice of cherry cake, would you eat the cake first or the cherry?"

But Man-Man didn't bother to answer Mo's question; instead, she wrote on a piece of paper:

Don't let your mind wander. Focus on your homework!

Man-Man pushed the piece of paper on to Mo's desk.

What a spoilsport! Mo thought.

Mo knew it had been stupid to ask Man-Man. He sometimes forgot that Man-Man had been given the job of keeping an eye on him by Ms Qin. Every time Mo misbehaved in class, Man-Man would write down his piece of mischief in her little notebook.

Then Mo had an idea! He decided that the best person to ask would be Penguin. Since food was Penguin's favourite subject – and also a subject he was an expert in – he would definitely be able to answer the question.

Penguin sat right behind Mo. But just as Mo turned around to speak to Penguin, Ms Qin spotted him.

"Mo, what are you doing?" she demanded.

"I, um, I want to ask Penguin a homework problem," he mumbled.

"Ask who?" Ms Qin wasn't sure she heard it right. "You said you were going to ask Penguin?"

Some students began to giggle. Everyone knew that if Mo didn't know the answer to a homework problem, then Penguin *certainly* wouldn't know it.

"Mo, if you need to ask someone, ask Man-Man," Ms Qin said.

Man-Man waited for Mo to ask her about the problem. But Mo began drawing something on a piece of paper: first he drew a slice of cake, and then he drew a cherry on top of the cake; finally, he wrote:

Penguin, answer this: would you eat the cake first, or the cherry?

After making sure Ms Qin wasn't watching, Mo crumpled the piece of paper into a ball and threw it on to Penguin's desk.

Penguin giggled when he read the piece of paper.

"Penguin, what are you giggling about?" asked Ms Qin.

Nothing escape Ms Qin's eagle-eyes. Penguin immediately stopped giggling and carried on writing.

Ms Qin smiled. She thought Penguin had gone back to his homework; but in fact, Penguin was writing on the piece of paper Mo had thrown to him.

Penguin wrote:

I wouldn't eat the cherry first, and I wouldn't eat the cake first either. I would bury the cherry inside the cake and then eat them both at the same time!

Seeing that Ms Qin was looking elsewhere, Penguin crumpled the piece of paper into a ball again, and tried throwing it back to Mo. But instead, the piece of paper landed on the desk of the child sitting in front of Mo – Monkey.

Monkey had already finished his homework and was just wondering what to do next. The flying paper ball was a pleasant surprise, and he shrieked as the paper landed on his desk.

"Monkey, stop shrieking," Ms Qin said.

Monkey quickly shut up.

Ms Qin nodded in approval.

Monkey began drawing on the piece of paper that Penguin had thrown over: he drew a cherry tree growing out of the slice of cake, and the tree was full of cherries.

After Monkey had finished his drawing, he threw the paper to Hippo. But Hippo sat two desks away from Monkey and Monkey missed his target. Hippo had to stand up and pick the paper up from the floor.

"Hippo, what are you doing standing up?" asked Ms Qin. She was relieved that it wasn't Penguin standing up, because she knew what *he* would have been up to – and she didn't want any farting during Homework time!

Hippo quickly sat down.

Ms Qin was satisfied, and she turned her attention away again.

Hippo began drawing on the piece of paper Monkey had thrown to him: he drew cherries falling from the cherry tree and they all landed in the cake. The cake was covered with ripe cherries.

Hippo threw the piece of paper back to Mo.

The piece of paper had now been passed between the four boys before it finally came back to Mo. Mo happily discovered that they'd found a solution to his problem. On the paper, Hippo had written:

As there are now so many cherries, it is no longer a problem whether to eat the cherry first or to eat the cake first. You can have a bite of the cake, and then eat a cherry, then another bite of the cake, and then another cherry, and so on.

Now that was teamwork!

AFTER SCHOOL

Every day, on his way home from school, Mo and the other boys walked through a community park. Recently, a new luxury public toilet, built in traditional Chinese style, had been put up in the park. Though Mo and his gang had once held a secret meeting *outside* the public toilet, the boys, who were always very curious about new things, wanted to check it out *inside*.

"What is there to check out?" Penguin wasn't particularly interested in seeing inside a public toilet. Penguin had seen lots of extravagant toilets in five-star hotels when he travelled with his dad. "It's just a place for peeing," he said.

"But I wonder if I would really be able to pee if I was inside such an expensive-looking toilet?" said Mo. "What if I was too nervous because it was so posh in there?" He was determined to try it out for himself.

The luxury public toilet was beautifully constructed with a traditional curved front gate. On one side of the gate, there was an office with a desk and chair in it.

"Hey look, this toilet even has an office!" exclaimed Mo.

Mo was just about to step inside the front gate when a large woman blocked his way.

"Just a minute! Where do you think you're all going?" she asked the boys.

"We're going to the Men's Room, not the Ladies' Room. Why are you stopping us?" Mo asked.

"You need to pay first." The large woman pointed to the fee written on a sign. "Fifty cents per person. There are four of you, so you need to pay two yuan."

"But we're not going to pee. We just want to take a look inside," said Hippo.

The fat woman stared at the boys. "Not going to pee?' Then what's there to look at?"

"Do we still have to pay even if we don't pee?"

Penguin was quite good at haggling.

"Yes. Pee or no pee, you have to pay if you want to go inside."

"Can you give us a discount? Say, 50% off?"

The woman was not impressed.

Penguin tried again. "How about 40% off? 30%? 30% is our final offer, we can't pay a cent more."

"What an annoying kid you are!"

The large woman started to shoo them away. "Stop wasting my time if you can't pay!"

"Who says we can't pay?!" Mo took out two one yuan coins and banged them on the desk.

Once she saw the coins, the woman stopped shooing them away. She sat down in front of the desk, took out a bunch of keys from her suit pocket, and unlocked a drawer. Then she put the two coins into the drawer and gave four tickets to Mo and the boys. "And don't misbehave in there," she said.

"Let's go, guys!" Mo signalled for everyone to follow him. "To the luxury toilet, my treat!" Mo sounded very excited.

But just as the four boys were about to step inside, the woman yelled at them to hold their horses.

"We've already paid!" The boys argued.

"I know. But that door is the Ladies' Room." The woman pointed to the symbol of a high-heeled shoe on the door.

"The Men's Room is over there." The woman then pointed to the symbol of a tobacco pipe on the door of the Men's Room.

The boys felt a bit embarrassed. Monkey quickly counter-attacked and asked the woman. "Why don't you just write *Men's Room* on the door? Why a tobacco pipe? It's stupid."

"Tobacco pipes symbolise men, and high-heeled shoes symbolise women."

The woman pointed to her own feet: she was wearing a pair of high-heeled shoes.

"Why should a tobacco pipe symbolise men? " said Mo. "We're men and we don't smoke!"

The woman laughed and said, "Oh boys, you're not men yet! Just go in and pee! Go and pee and no mischief!" The woman hurriedly shooed the boys inside the Men's Room.

The Men's Room was very spacious, even bigger than the living room of Penguin's house. And there was a very pleasant smell in the air, not the usual smell of public toilets. Mo looked around and finally saw an aromatic oil burner underneath the sink.

Apart from the nice smell, the soft lighting added to the pleasant atmosphere. Mo looked everywhere but he couldn't find the source of the light. With such a high-tech lighting system, no wonder this toilet charged an entrance fee.

"Ready?

Monkey and the other boys decided to have a peeing contest. This was one of the boys' favourite activities. They'd had the contest on top of hills, competing to see who could pee the furthest; they'd had the contest around trees to see who could pee the highest; and on the beach, to see who could make the biggest patch of wet sand! This time, they decided to see who could pee the loudest.

"Go!"

The boys all listened intently to see who was making the loudest sound.

Suddenly they heard the noise of a toilet flushing. They hadn't realised anyone else was in the public toilet. They stopped their noise and started to pee normally. A man rushed out of a cubicle, washed his hands quickly and scuttled out.

But in his rush, the man dropped something – an envelope!

Monkey picked up the envelope and, as it wasn't sealed, he peeked inside and took out a CD.

Mo and the boys rushed out of the toilet to chase after the man.

"Hey, Mister! Wait!"

But the man thought the boys were going to make trouble and he quickly got into his Mercedes Benz and drove away.

REWARDS

Now the boys had a mission. It was up to them to return the envelope with the CD in it to the man.

Mo had an idea as to who the man might be. The Mercedes was a clue.

"I think he looks like a politician," Mo said. "He was in a hurry and he had a very expensive car."

"Politicians don't drive Mercedes. They drive Audis," Penguin said.

Penguin knew all about cars. He said, "Men who drive Mercedes are usually owners of big companies."

Then Mo had an another idea! He took a look at the

envelope and saw there were two lines written on the front. One line said: *Kingdom Real Estate*, and the second line said: *For the attention of Mr Jason Zheng, CEO*.

That man must be Jason Zheng – the CEO of Kingdom Real Estate!

Mo held up the CD and asked the boys, "What do you think is on this CD?"

"Not computer games, I'll bet," said Penguin.

But Mo hoped the disk *did* contain computer games. "How can you be so sure?" he asked Penguin.

"You must remember, my dad is a CEO too," Penguin said. "If this CD belongs to a CEO, it must be something very important."

The boys all agreed with Penguin. And if the disk was that important, they must return it to Mr Jason Zheng the CEO of Kingdom Real Estate!

But no one knew where Kingdom Real Estate was. Although the address was written on the envelope, none of the boys knew how to get there.

Mo had another idea. "We'll have to get a taxi," he said. "We could even say 'Follow that car!' like real detectives."

The four boys waved down a passing taxi. They

hopped in and showed the address to the driver. The driver knew the place, and the boys were on their way.

The taxi stopped right in front of a huge glass tower block. Above the entrance, in tall silver letters, was written *Kingdom Real Estate*. Penguin was the first to get out of the taxi, leaving the other boys to wonder how they were going to pay the fare. He walked straight towards the uniformed security guard with his hands folded behind his back and asked, "Is the CEO of your company named Jason Zheng?"

"Yes, he is," the guard nodded suspiciously. "Why do you want to know?"

"Ask him to come down and pay for our taxi fare," Penguin demanded.

The guard was about to push Penguin away. "You kids shouldn't be messing around here!"

The taxi driver overheard their conversation and asked, "What's going on? You boys haven't paid your fare yet."

"We haven't got any money," Penguin said. "We found something that belongs to the CEO of this company. So we want to return it to him. Don't you think *he* should be paying for our taxi fare?"

The taxi driver laughed. "I see. So you boys are

doing something nice. Well, in that case, I'll be nice too, just this once. You boys just got yourself a free ride."

The taxi driver drove away without collecting his fare.

"Mister, did you see that?" Monkey was trying to sweet talk their way into the building. "What a nice driver he is!"

The security guard saw the boys were holding an envelope with the CEO's name on it. He let them pass and even told them that the CEO's Office was on the 16th floor. "Make a right and it's the last room in the corridor," he told them.

They took the lift to the 16th floor and knocked on the door of the last room in the corridor.

"Come in!" a low voice said.

When Mo and the boys entered the room, they saw

that sitting behind a huge desk was the man they'd last seen getting into his Mercedes.

"What are you four boys doing here? Did you follow me?" he said, warily.

Monkey handed the envelope to Jason Zheng and said, "Is this yours?"

"Oh my goodness!" Jason Zheng drew in his breath. "Where did you find this? I have been searching for it everywhere."

"We found it in the public toilet. We were in there when you rushed out in a hurry."

"Of course, now I remember." Jason Zheng quickly cut the boys off, then said: "You have no idea how important that CD is. What can I do for you, in return?"

Mo desperately wanted a ride in the Mercedes Benz, so Mr Zheng rang all the boys' parents and asked if that would be all right. Penguin's father knew Mr Zheng through his business dealings, and said he was a good man. He reassured Monkey, Mo and Hippo's parents that their sons would be OK.

So the boys went for a ride in Jason Zheng's spacious Mercedes, which felt incredible! Mo said, "Mr Zheng, if you really want to reward us, could you

 69

take us for a fast ride on the motorway?"

"No problem!"

The Mercedes picked up speed and went as smoothly as if it had wings. Mo and the boys thought it was the coolest thing ever!

When they'd returned to the city, Jason Zheng stopped the car in front of a shopping mall and took the boys inside. He was going to buy a gift for them, a gift that all four boys could enjoy.

But choosing this gift proved very difficult. The four boys all wanted different things. No one could pick an item that everybody liked. The boys argued among themselves for a long time, and Jason Zheng thought he was about to go nuts.

"Stop! No more arguing. *I* will pick the gift."

Jason Zheng decided to buy them a tent.

"But how do we have fun with a tent, exactly?"

"This tent is big enough for all four of you when you go camping. It will be great fun!"

THE CAMPING PLAN

Jason Zheng had insisted on buying a tent for Mo and the boys because he had loved camping as a boy. At first, Mo and the boys weren't too enthusiastic about getting a tent. But Jason Zheng told them how much fun they could have: squeezing into the tent and spending a night in the wild; telling ghost stories and competing to see who could scream the loudest. Soon the boys were very excited about the idea of going camping.

But who would keep the tent and what would they tell their parents?

"Mo, why don't you take the tent home?" suggested Hippo.

But Penguin objected. "The tent is not just for Mo. It is for all four of us. So we can't let Mo take it."

Mo said, "The tent's got lots of parts. Why don't we divide them up and each take back a few?"

"No, definitely not!" said Monkey. He was more careful than the other three boys and he was thinking about something none of the other boys had thought of. "If we are going camping, we *have* to keep it a secret from our parents. So if we take any part of the tent home, they'll know about our camping plan."

Aha. Not even Mo had thought of that.

"So what do we do with the tent?" they said.

"Let's find a secret place and hide it," said Monkey.

The boys carried the tent and started to walk towards their homes. Finally, they were back in the place where they'd first seen Jason Zheng – at the luxury toilet. The toilet was in the middle of a small park and was surrounded by lots of trees.

The large lady who collected the toilet fee must have gone home. The door to the toilet was locked and there was no one around. It was a perfect place to hide the tent, but where?

Then Mo had an idea! "Let's bury the tent," he suggested.

The boys bent down and dug a hole with their hands. They put the tent in the hole, put the earth back on top and stamped on it to make the ground flat. Finally, they placed a few rocks on top to make it look more natural.

Now that the boys had a real secret to keep, they were always whispering together at school. Man-Man wanted to know what was going on, so she could write down any mischief in her little notebook.

The boys had been discussing their camping plan, such as when and where it would take place, what to take – especially food – and how to keep it a secret from their parents.

Since Monkey sat in front of Mo, and Penguin sat behind him, it was very difficult for Mo, who sat next to Man-Man, to pretend he had nothing to hide. Mo wasn't very good at keeping secrets.

"Monkey, what if it rains?" Mo asked.

Man-Man was trying hard to hear what was being said.

Monkey turned round and glanced at Man-Man, then winked at Mo. "Even if it rains, there's nothing to worry about. Don't you remember? We have *the thing*."

Monkey quickly made an outline with his hands and Mo knew he was talking about their tent.

But Man-Man didn't understand what Monkey was doing. She grew even more suspicious.

A moment later, Mo thought about something else and turned round and asked Penguin, "Penguin, what if they call the police?"

Again, Man-Man was desperate to hear what they were plotting.

"Call the police?" Penguin didn't get it at first. "What are you talking about?"

"If our parents can't find us, do you think they will call the police?"

When Man-Man heard 'parents can't find us', she quickly took out her notebook and wrote down this important piece of information.

After school was over, Man-Man ran to Ms Qin's office as fast as she could and reported what she'd heard. Ms Qin ran out of her office and caught Mo at the bottom of the staircase and brought him back to her office.

"Mo, what are you up to now?"

"I'm not up to anything," he said, smiling sweetly.

"Are you trying to run away from home?" asked Ms Qin.

Mo remembered what he'd said earlier in class. He knew Man-Man must have overheard the conversation.

"Ms Qin, I was just kidding. I wouldn't really run

away from home, I was just *imagining* what might happen."

"Oh, really?"

Ms Qin's stare was sharp and penetrating. Mo couldn't bring himself to look at her.

Ms Qin didn't ask anything else, she just kept staring at Mo. Mo was growing so uneasy under Ms Qin's stare that he didn't know quite what to do. Fortunately, Mo was saved by the bell so he quickly returned to the classroom.

After Mo had left, Ms Qin thought very carefully about what he had said. She didn't think that Mo would really run away from home, because he had a very happy family. But she was a very responsible and very experienced teacher, and she was very reliable too. To be on the safe side, she phoned Mo's father and told him about her concerns.

Although Ms Qin had questioned Mo in her office that day, it wasn't going to change the boys' camping plan. Mo was always going to Ms Qin's office about something or other, so he didn't think there was a problem. *Not* being called to Ms Qin's office on any given day, now *that* would be strange!

The camping trip was planned for Friday evening.

The boys were going to leave a note for their parents after they'd got home from school on Friday. Then, they would take food and any items needed for the night and meet up at the luxury public toilet. There, they would dig up the tent, and then take the train to Fresh Meadow Park just outside the city.

Nothing could possibly go wrong…

HiDE AND SEEK

On Friday afternoon, after Mo had got home from school, he took out the note he had prepared and stuck it on the fridge door. Monkey had written the letter and all the boys had copied it. This is what it said:

Dear Mum and Dad,

I will not be home tonight. Please do not worry about me and please do not try to find me. I promise I will come home safe and sound tomorrow. Please just let me have one night of freedom.

Your son

The boys wanted to leave a note because they didn't want their parents worrying about them. And they especially didn't want their parents calling the police!

Mo filled a rucksack with food and other equipment. Then he left home.

Mo had *absolutely* no idea that as soon as he left home, someone else left too – his dad!

A few days ago, Ms Qin had called Mo's father to tell him about her suspicions. Since then, Mo's father had been paying close attention to Mo's every move. Mo was hopeless at keeping secrets, and when his dad noticed how excited his son had been acting lately, he knew Mo was up to something!

Mo's father felt even more excited about Mo running away from home than Mo himself. He phoned Hippo's father, Penguin's father and Monkey's father and told them about the boys' plan to run away from home. The four boys had been friends since childhood. Whenever they got into trouble together, their fathers would be called to school. So the four fathers had known each other for quite some time too. Having children who were mischievous was something they all had in common, and talking about their mischievous kids had made the four fathers good friends.

Mo's father told the other three fathers that their sons might be "missing" this weekend. He suggested that they follow their sons. All the fathers felt very excited about this plan. What could be more fun than a little game of "hide and seek" between fathers and sons?

As he was following his son, Mo's dad rang Hippo's father, Penguin's father and Monkey's father on his mobile.

"Are you on your way too?"

"Yes, I'm on my way."

"Good, don't let him out of your sight."

"Got it. I'll call you later."

But following their sons proved a demanding task. They had to make sure they were well hidden from the boys, and they were getting a little tired keeping up with the youngsters. Then the boys reached their destination. The fathers were surprised to see that their sons were meeting outside a public toilet. What on earth were they up to?

The large woman in charge of colleting entrance fees was still at work. As soon as the four boys arrived, they could feel the woman's gaze on them. They had to wait until she went home before they could dig up their tent.

Seeing the four boys hanging around the public toilet, the large woman thought that maybe they were going to pee in the trees surrounding the toilet.

"Hey, if you pee in public, I will have to fine you!" she yelled at the boys.

"What makes you think we're here to pee?"

"If you're not here to pee, then what are you doing hanging around a toilet?"

"Why *can't* we hang around the toilet even if we are not here to pee?" Monkey challenged the woman.

The woman didn't know what to say to the boys. She was so angry that she started hiccupping so she couldn't speak at all. And since she couldn't shoo the boys away, she decided she would leave work early.

So she locked up the toilet and went home.

As soon as the large woman left, the four boys dug up the tent and carried it to the nearby subway station. But the fathers couldn't see what the boys had dug up. They were more curious than ever!

The fathers followed their sons to the subway station. The boys bought tickets, went through the barriers, then hopped on to a train. The fathers did the same.

"What on earth did they dig up?" asked Monkey's father.

Mo's father was the only one who had a pretty good idea about what that thing was. Since he was a toy designer and spent loads of time around toys and gadgets, it was easy for him to tell just by its shape.

"It looked like a tent to me, a camping tent in a bag."

"That tent must have been expensive," said Monkey's father. "Where did they get the money to buy it? I hope they didn't steal it."

Penguin's father was very good at guessing prices. "A tent like that must have cost at least 2000 or 3000 yuan," he said.

Hippo's father was more interested in finding out what the boys intended to do with the tent.

As the train travelled out of the city, there were fewer and fewer passengers on it. The boys were messing around in the train. Monkey was acting like a monkey. Penguin was waddling round the carriage like a penguin. Hippo was laughing, his mouth wide open. Mo was just laughing. When the train had been crowded, it had been easier for the fathers to blend in. Now there were fewer passengers, their sons could easily see them, so the fathers took out their newspapers and covered their faces, pretending to be reading.

When the train reached the last stop, the boys got out of the train, and the fathers followed, still covering their faces with newspapers.

"Hey, did you notice those weird guys?" said Monkey. "Have you ever seen people reading newspapers while walking?"

Monkey was the cleverest of the four boys. He turned around and was surprised to see that the four guys who were reading newspapers had suddenly vanished from sight. The four fathers had realised that Monkey was suspicious and now they were all hiding underneath a long bench!

"I think we are being followed!" said Monkey.

"What? Who could be following us?" said the others.

Mo thought this was SO exciting. He looked around so see who was following.

"I can't see anybody following us, I think you're just seeing things, Monkey," he said. "You've watched too many episodes of CSI."

"No, seriously, I saw four guys hiding their faces behind newspapers."

"He's right!" Penguin remembered seeing those guys too. "When we were on the train, there *were* some people covering their faces with newspapers."

"That means ... we ARE being followed! Let's hurry up!" Hippo picked up the tent and headed towards the subway exit.

The exit was straight ahead. Fresh Meadow Park was towards the left of the exit, but Monkey told Hippo to take the path on the right.

"Why? Fresh Meadow Park isn't that way."

"Don't you get it? We're going to trick whoever is following us."

Mo got it straightaway. He led the gang and headed towards the right.

The fathers all heard footsteps towards the right side of the subway exit. So they headed quietly towards the right side.

But as soon as the boys got out of the exit, they immediately circled back on to the left path. The fathers had been tricked. They continued heading towards the right.

Mo and the boys arrived at Fresh Meadow Park. But

the fathers were still wandering around near the subway exit. The area was like a labyrinth, all the buildings and roads looked exactly the same, and the fathers couldn't find their way out.

SCREAMS IN THE TENT

Fresh Meadow Park wasn't the kind of park that was surrounded by fences and walls. Neither did it charge an entrance fee, so the boys knew they didn't have to worry about being driven out by park rangers at night. Fresh Meadow Park was more of a forest than a park, and there were plenty of places to camp.

Mo and the boys kept looking back over their shoulders as they ran further into the park, making sure they'd got rid of whoever was following them.

"I think we've lost them!" Monkey cheered.

But Mo didn't think getting rid of their followers was something worth cheering about. For him, having someone on their trail was exciting!

"I hope those people can keep up with us," Mo said. "If we play hide and seek with them in this forest, we're bound to win."

Hide and seek was Hippo and Penguin's favourite game as well. The boys now all blamed Monkey for thinking of a way to get rid of their followers.

"Hide and seek? You guys are out of your mind! If those people were the police, they would have captured us and taken us home. And if those people were bad people, our lives would probably be in danger!" Monkey slashed his finger across his neck and rolled his eyes back.

The boys realised that having someone following them could be dangerous and that it was no joke.

Penguin was a bit worried now. "Hey, Monkey, do you think whoever was following us is still following us?"

"Of course they're not. We got rid of them. I'm sure they're already on the subway back to the city." Monkey looked his watch. "It's almost eight o'clock. If they're not on the subway right now, they've missed the last train, hah!"

Everyone thought about what Monkey had said and it made sense. So the boys started feeling a bit more relaxed. They were convinced that the people who'd been following them must have got on the last train, so were well on their way back to the city.

But the people who *were* following them – Mo's father, Hippo's father, Monkey's father and Penguin's father – were still trying to figure their way out of the labyrinth of streets around the subway exit.

Monkey's father was just like his son – quick to come up with a solution. "I think the kids tricked us. They didn't take the right-hand path in the first place."

"So how did we end up here in this labyrinth?" Penguin's father was just like *his* son – always complaining when things didn't go right.

Hippo's father was also just like his son – more heavily built than the other dads and a little slow. "But I saw them heading this way with my own eyes!"

Mo's father was like his son too – he always found the fun in everything, and never gave up. "I'm sure they took the exit on the right and then circled back to the path on the left."

"You're right!" A light bulb switched on in Hippo's dad's brain. "Fresh Meadow Park is to the left when you come out of the subway. I've brought Hippo to this park before."

The four fathers hurriedly headed towards the park.

The sun had already set. It was getting late and the moon couldn't be seen; there were just a few stars twinkling in the evening sky.

The four fathers were now walking in the forest. A thick canopy of trees had blocked out the weak light from the few stars and they felt like they were inside a large house with no lights on.

"Ouch!" Monkey's father ran right into a tree and immediately got a big lump on his forehead.

"Look what we have to go through because of our kids!" Penguin's father dragged his feet with difficulty and panted heavily to try to catch his breath.

"Quiet," Mo's father put a finger to his lips. "Listen, can you hear something?"

The fathers stopped and listened very carefully. There was the sound of laughter from somewhere quite near.

The fathers held each other's arms in the darkness and tried to find their way towards the sound.

Soon, they could see a light. The light came from inside a tent, where the laughter was also coming from.

"There it is – the tent!" Mo's father sounded very excited. "Our boys are all in the tent!"

It was true – their sons were all in the tent. The fathers were very close. They could even tell now which one of the boys was talking at that moment.

"What now?" Hippo's father kept his voice low. "What do we do now?"

"What else?!" Penguin's father kept his voice low. "We take them back right now!"

"No!" said Mo's father. He sounded like he had already made up his mind about what to do. "Listen to how happy they are right now!"

"You're right. We really shouldn't ruin their fun!" Monkey's father sighed. "Childhood was much more fun in our day."

The fathers decided to set up their own camp behind a large rock. They didn't have a tent, of course, but at least they could have a small campfire. They gathered up some twigs and branches and, using

Penguin's father's cigarette lighter, lit the fire. Then they all settled round the campfire and started to tell stories of their childhoods. They kept their voices very low and muffled their laughter.

It started to rain, but they didn't mind. Fathers *and* sons were having a great time!

In the tent, Mo was telling a ghost story. The raindrops pattering on the tent made the story even spookier.

The tent had a little window. Mo was just talking about how ghosts lit fires in graveyards. Penguin looked outside through the little window and thought he saw a fire flickering in the distance.

"Ahh!" Penguin screamed. "I saw the ghosts' fire!"

Hippo, Monkey and Mo leaped to the window and stared into the darkness. It was true, they all saw the ghosts' fire flickering.

"Ahh—Ahh—Ahh—!!"

The boys began screaming at the same time. Mo had told them before that screaming could scare away ghosts.

What the boys thought was the ghosts' fire was only the glow from the fathers' campfire! When the fathers heard the boys screaming, they stamped on their campfire to put it out, then rushed towards the tent, thinking their sons were in trouble.

But the boys' screams died down when the glow from the campfire disappeared. Mo had an idea!

"Hey, let's have a screaming contest!"

Mo's suggestion was very well received. The boys screamed even louder than before.

The fathers were no longer worried when they knew their sons were having a screaming contest. They started laughing, and they didn't have to worry about muffling their voices anymore, because the boys would never hear them. And, because they were no longer worried about their sons, they lit another campfire and all settled down to more storytelling. They could be children again for just one night!

THREE STINGY FRIENDS

The children of Class 4Q were going on a trip to the Botanical Garden.

Ms Qin asked all the children to take pencils and notebooks as well as a packed lunch.

"Why do we need pencils and notebooks?" asked Mo. "We're going for a day trip, not a lesson, aren't we?"

"Mo, why do you *always* have to say something?" Ms Qin was in a good mood, so she wasn't going to let herself get mad at Mo and went on, "The Botanical Garden has many rare plants. I want you to write down in your notebook the names of all of these plants and any additional information you can find about them. You will be writing a report when you get back to school."

"Write down *all* of them? We won't have any time to play!" Seeing that Ms Qin was in a good mood, Mo started pushing his luck.

"Mo, is playing the only thing that's ever on your mind?" Ms Qin still wasn't mad, so she went on, "The schedule for tomorrow will be as follows: the morning will be group activity, and the afternoon will be individual activity."

Mo knew that "individual activity" meant free time for playing. He would have an entire afternoon for having fun!

After dinner, Mo's dad took him to the supermarket and filled a trolley with food for Mo to take on the trip.

"You'll never eat that much, Mo!" laughed his father.

"It's not all for me, Dad. If, say, some of my

classmates don't like their own food and they ask if I will share mine, I will be able to. If, say, some of my classmates forget to bring their own food, then I can share mine with them. If, say —"

"All right, all right, that's enough!"

If Mo's dad had let Mo go on, Mo would have come up with hundreds of reasons for taking so much food. Deep down, his dad was very proud of Mo for being such a generous boy. Mo wasn't stingy, like Penguin, Mo was a caring, sharing sort of boy.

But Mo couldn't possibly stuff all the food in his schoolbag. So he had to use his rucksack, the one he'd used for the camping trip.

The next day Mo carried his rucksack, full of food, to school.

Ms Qin was quite taken aback by the rucksack. "Mo, are you going camping again?"

The whole class started laughing.

Mo didn't see what there was to laugh about.

Ms Qin opened Mo's rucksack and saw that it was full of food. "Mo, I am totally speechless," she cried.

On the school bus, the children sang all the way to the

Botanical Garden, which was located in the suburbs of the city.

Once they'd arrived, they began a tour of the garden.

"Now, please take out your pencils and notebooks and take notes as we go round."

Everyone took out a pencil and notebook, except for Mo. He'd been so busy packing food into his rucksack, he had forgotten to put his pencil and notebook in too.

"Mo, where are your pencil and your notebook?"

"I … I forgot them."

"How come you didn't forget to bring your food?"

Ms Qin was getting a little cross this time. "Tell me, what you are here for?"

"To have fun," Monkey answered for Mo. The whole class burst out laughing again.

Ms Qin knew it was simply a waste of time to stay cross with Mo. She took out her own pencil and notebook and handed them to Mo.

As the children walked round the Botanical Garden, they took down notes about the plants, herbs and shrubs that they saw. Mo was very careful about the notes he took because his pencil and notebook were from Ms Qin. He took down three whole pages full of notes and did some drawings too.

After the tour was over, it was time to have lunch.

"Where's my rucksack?" gasped Mo. He held the pencil in one hand and the notebook in the other.

The other children had put their lunch in their schoolbags. Mo's rucksack had been on his back. It was heavy and he remembered taking

it off to take down some notes. But then Ms Qin called them to look at something else and he'd left his rucksack where he'd put it down. He just couldn't remember where that somewhere was…

All of his classmates were having lunch. Mo was hungry and he was the only one without any food to eat. But he did have three best buddies to rely on!

Mo went to Monkey first. Monkey was very skinny and didn't eat much, so he was bound to share some of his food with Mo.

"You can forget about getting food from *me*," said Monkey. "Look at me, I'm already skinny. How could you have the heart to ask for food from *me*?" Monkey called Mo closer and whispered, "Let me tell you something, Penguin brought four hamburgers, four fried drumsticks and—"

So Mo asked Penguin if he would share his food with him.

"Well Mo, I know we're good friends but I have a very big tummy, so I have to eat four hamburgers and four drumsticks to fill it." Penguin sounded nervous. He covered his schoolbag with both hands as if Mo was going to rob him of his fried drumsticks and hamburgers.

Mo's last hope lay with Hippo, who was bigger and taller than either Monkey or Penguin.

Hippo sounded very sorry. "Mo, I've only brought two hamburgers and two fried drumsticks. It's only just enough for me. You know, if I'm hungry, I get a bit faint."

Mo was fed up. How dare those three call themselves his friends? How dare they say they were his *best buddies*? They wouldn't even share their lunch with him! Mo had had enough of these so-called friends.

Mo ran off. He couldn't let his three stingy friends see how upset he was.

But Mo didn't stay fed up for long. He was determined to find his lost rucksack. If he could find his rucksack, he would eat everything in it, in front of the three stingy so-called friends. They could beg all they wanted and he wouldn't let them have anything. Not ONE crumb.

The more Mo thought about it, the more he cheered up. Mo imagined his three stingy so-called friends drooling over his rucksack of tasty food that they would never get to try. Mo laughed out loud and even did a few somersaults!

FOOD TREES

The Botanical Garden was a huge place.

Mo was still searching for his rucksack packed with food. But he got lost and ended up in an area where there was not a single visitor in sight.

"Is there anyone around?" Mo yelled out loud. "Somebody! Anybody!"

The place was so quiet that it was spooky.

"Is anybody here? Somebody—"

Suddenly, someone muffled Mo's mouth from behind and pressed him down to the ground.

"Shut up!" said a sinister voice. "Keep on yelling and you're dead!"

Mo didn't dare make another sound. He turned around and saw an evil-looking man with a very stubbly chin.

Mo was scared. This man looked nasty.

"Kid, what did you see?" the stubbly man questioned Mo.

"I saw what you were doing—"

Mo was bluffing. He hadn't seen anything, he was far too busy looking for his rucksack.

Stubbly Chin demanded, "Did you see me taking those pots of fragrant thoroughwort?"

Mo gasped. The man had been trying to steal fragrant thoroughwort – Mo had just learned that fragrant thoroughwort was a very valuable herb.

"I didn't see anything! Honestly! Please let me go!"

"No, I can't let you go yet." Stubbly Chin dragged Mo towards a tree. "I'm going to tie you up to that tree. I'll let you go after I finish with my business."

Stubbly Chin tied Mo to the tree and warned him to stay quiet.

Mo decided he'd better obey. He was only a boy and the man looked strong.

Mo watched as Stubbly Chin moved the pots of fragrant thoroughwort to the bottom of the wall that surrounded the Botanical Garden. Stubbly Chin placed a ladder against the wall. He picked up a tub of fragrant thoroughwort, climbed on to the ladder, and carefully placed the tub on top of the wall. He repeated what he'd done until all the tubs of fragrant thoroughwort were on top of the wall.

Mo knew that Stubbly Chin was going to climb over the wall using the ladder, then take the tubs of fragrant thoroughwort one by one from the top of the wall, down the other side and out of the garden.

And he was already half-way there.

Stubbly Chin had already moved the ladder so it was on the other side of the wall. And he had started on his first journey down the other side with one tub of Thoroughwort.

"THIEF!" Mo suddenly started screaming. "THIEF, STOP THIEF!"

Meanwhile, Hippo, Monkey and Penguin were

looking for Mo. They were feeling a bit guilty about not sharing their food with him. The boys had also lost their way and ended up not too far from the tree where Mo was tied up. Mo's screams were loud and clear. They ran towards the sound.

"STOP THIEF! STOP THIEF!"

"If you keep on screaming, I'll kill you!" yelled Stubbly Chin, threatening Mo from the other side of the wall.

"STOP THIEF! STOP THIEF!" Mo wasn't going to give up.

"Mo!" Hippo and the others had found Mo. "What's going on? Why are you tied up?"

"Someone's trying to steal the fragrant thoroughwort."

"Where?" Penguin looked around and couldn't see anyone.

"He's hiding on the other side of the wall." The boys untied Mo, and Mo started to give them orders. "Monkey, go and tell someone right now. Hippo and Penguin, arm yourselves!"

"Arm … arm ourselves? But what with?!"

"Yeah, we don't have anything to arm ourselves with." Monkey ran to call someone.

"Let's arm ourselves with rocks!"

Mo picked up a stone. "Didn't you guys used to brag about how great you were at hitting targets with rocks? Well, now's the time to prove you can do it. That thief is all yours!"

The boys found an ideal spot to launch their attack. Hippo and Penguin found lots of rocks and stacked them up.

Stubbly Chin was still hiding on the other side of the wall and didn't hear anyone coming. He thought the coast was clear and that it was safe to climb back up to the top of the wall. He wanted to finish stealing the remaining tubs of fragrant thoroughwort.

"Attack!" As soon as the boys saw the thief coming up the other side of the wall, Mo gave the order.

It started raining rocks. One rock hit Stubbly Chin right on the chest, the other on the shoulder. He quickly ducked his head back down the other side of the wall. The boys kept on throwing more rocks, to make sure he didn't come back.

Just as the boys' attack stopped, Monkey rushed back with two security guards. Mo told them about what had happened and that one tub of fragrant thoroughwort was already over the other side of the wall.

One of the security guards quickly climbed over the wall and found the tub of fragrant thoroughwort on the ground safe and sound, together with the ladder. The thief was nowhere to be seen.

"Well done, you boys. These tubs of fragrant thoroughwort are the most expensive kind, worth hundreds of thousands of yuan!"

"Hundreds of thousands of yuan?!" Monkey winked and said, "Does this mean we're all heroes for protecting national property?!"

The security guards thought this was very funny, and smiled.

Penguin quickly told the guards their names, "I am Penguin, he's Mo, this guy here is Hippo, and he's Monkey. Please write a letter to our school telling them what happened."

The security guards thought this was even funnier and promised the boys that they would write a letter to their school. Then the guards busied themselves putting the stolen herbs back where they belonged.

On their way back to the rest of their class, Mo asked the boys, "How did you guys find me?"

"We found a tree," said Penguin. "There was lots of tasty food growing in it."

"What??!" Mo was starving. A tree with tasty food growing in it sounded good to him!

Mo followed the boys and there it was! A tree with lots of tasty food sitting in its branches: fried drumsticks, hamburgers, cake, potato crisps, grapes, jelly, yoghurt...

Mo was too hungry to wonder how all the food had got there. He grabbed a drumstick from the tree and took a bite. Then Penguin, Monkey and Hippo followed and they all had a feast.

What Mo couldn't have known was that his three best buddies weren't really being stingy earlier. It was Monkey who came up with the idea, as Mo was running around looking for his rucksack. Monkey persuaded the others to put some of their food in the tree. Then they waited and waited for Mo to come back so they could share their food with him. But Mo was nowhere to be seen... so his four friends went to look for him. And because of that they stopped a thief – they were all heroes!

BREAKING NEWS

It had been several days since the trip to the Botanical Garden. Mo and the boys had hoped that someone from the Botanical Garden would have sent a letter to school to say what heroes they had been. But so far, there was no news.

"Maybe they don't know our names," said Mo.

"Yes they do," Penguin said. "I told the guards our names. I said 'my name is Penguin, his name is Mo, his is Penguin and that is Monkey'."

Yes, that was right. Mo remembered. Penguin *had*

told the security guards their names, all four of them, right on the spot.

"Did you also tell them which school we were from? And which class?" asked Monkey.

"No, I didn't," cried Penguin.

Everyone blamed Penguin for not telling the security guards their school and their class.

"Why is it all my fault?" Penguin objected. "We've all got tongues, why didn't *you* say something to the guards?"

Penguin was right. So the boys stopped blaming everything on him.

But still, they didn't feel it was quite fair. After all, they had helped prevent the theft of herbs worth hundreds of thousands of yuan – one of the security guards had told them himself. Mo had even been tied up to a tree by the thief. They were all heroes and everyone should know about it.

After stopping the thief, Mo and the boys had sat under the food tree, enjoying the drumsticks, hamburgers, fruit jellies, crisps and yoghurt they picked from the branches. They decided they were going to be big heroes, but they wanted it to be a real scoop for someone.

"We should keep the fact that we became heroes today a secret for now. We can't tell anyone about it yet," Monkey said.

"Why?"

"Well, if we tell everyone now, it will be like a time-bomb blowing up ahead of time."

"What?" asked Mo. "What does that mean?"

"We mustn't tell the others now. Then when the letter arrives at school, it will be like a bomb – an explosive piece of news! Everyone will be AMAZED!"

So that's what Monkey had in mind! He was always as quick as a monkey. The boys thought what Monkey said made very good sense. The Gang of Four were already quite famous in school – famous for being naughty! They hoped that the "time-bomb"– the letter – would change their reputation from bad to good.

Then Mo had an idea! "But if no letter arrives at school, then *we* will tell the others about our heroic deeds."

And because no letter had arrived, that was what they were going to do.

Monkey and Penguin first spoke to Man-Man.

"Man-Man, that notebook of yours shouldn't just be used to write down Mo's *wrongdoings*, you should write down Mo's heroic deeds in that notebook too," said Monkey.

Man-Man asked: "Heroic deeds? What heroic deeds?"

"I'll tell you," said Penguin. "But of course, it wasn't just Mo who was heroic. It was all four of us, me, Hippo and Monkey too."

"A heroic act involving all four of you?" Man-Man wasn't buying this. She turned around and asked Lily, "Do you believe this?"

Lily didn't say whether she believed it or not; instead, she asked the boys to tell them about their heroic act.

So Monkey went on in his usual way, "It happened on that fateful day, when we went to the Botanical Garden. There he was, a scoundrel trying to steal the invaluable fragrant thoroughwort. We had a life-and-death confrontation with the scoundrel, and in the end, we successfully prevented national property from falling into the wrong hands."

Both Man-Man and Lily began to laugh. Lily laughed so hard that she had tears in her eyes.

"The fragrant thoroughwort was worth hundreds of thousands of yuan, which means we prevented the loss of a fortune for the Botanic Garden!" said Penguin.

"What a very *interesting* story that was, Monkey," said Man-Man.

"Couldn't you have made it a bit more believable?" joined in Lily.

Then Wen got to hear about it.

"You're not heroes, you're jokers!" he sneered.

"We ARE heroes," shouted Penguin.

"Yes, we ARE," joined in Hippo and Mo.

"We are the HEROES, we are the HEROES," shouted all four boys..

They were shouting so loudly that Ms Qin came out of her office to see what was going on.

So Man-Man told her what the boys had told her.

But Ms Qin didn't believe in their "hero" story, either.

"If what you said is true, why didn't tell me on the day of the trip?"

Ms Qin knew that if the boys really had done such a heroic act, they would have made sure the whole world knew by now.

Hippo told Ms Qin everything. "It was Monkey who said that we should keep it a secret."

 115

"Why would you want to keep such an act a secret?" Ms Qin couldn't understand it.

"We wanted to wait until the Botanical Garden sent a letter to the school."

"So where *is* this letter?"

"It's all Penguin's fault. He forgot to tell them which school we were from."

Ms Qin was beginning to believe him. Although Hippo had done a lot of mischievous deeds in the past, he didn't lie. Ms Qin knew that Hippo was an honest boy.

Hippo was about to cry. He was so afraid that Ms Qin wouldn't believe him.

"Ms Qin, why don't you call the Botanical Garden?"

Of course! If she telephoned them, then the truth would be revealed!

HONOURING LiTTLE HEROS

Ms Qin immediately called the Botanical Garden and asked whether someone had stolen some tubs of fragrant thoroughwort.

"*Attempted* to steal," the person at the Botanical Garden corrected Ms Qin. "Thanks to some boys who were on a school trip, the thief's attempt failed."

"Do you know the names of these boys?" Ms Qin pressed on.

"I don't know their names. But the security guards might."

One of the security guards who'd spoken to the boys picked up the phone. He told Ms Qin that none of them could quite remember the names. Only that they thought one of the boys was called Mo.

It had to be Mo Shen Ma!

But Ms Qin wanted to be sure. "Can you describe the boys?"

"One had a really wide mouth; one was very skinny; one was very chubby; the last one was neither skinny nor chubby, but he looked very mischievous."

Ms Qin sighed with relief. It had to be the four boys in her class.

The security guard told Ms Qin that they had wanted to send a letter to the school, praising the boys for their bravery, but they didn't know where to send it. Ms Qin told them the school's name and address.

The next day, a letter in a bright red envelope was delivered to Ms Qin at the school.

Ms Qin ran all the way to the head-teacher's office, panting for breath.

"Head-teacher …"

"Ms Qin, calm down, catch your breath first."

Ms Qin was so happy that she was speechless for a moment. She handed the head-teacher the letter.

"That's wonderful. Your hard work has paid off!" The head-teacher completely understood how Ms Qin felt. Indeed, she felt the same way too. "Ms Qin, I know how much time and effort you have spent on those four boys. They had the courage to stick up for what is right and to confront evil. This is proof that your teaching has been successful. Your effort with them has not gone in vain."

What the head-teacher said was exactly how Ms

Qin felt. It had all been worth it, after all.

The head-teacher then said, "If it had been our best behaved and brightest children who had saved the valuable plants, then just a little praise would be enough. But since it was children whose behaviour we want to improve, then we must reward their good behaviour. We must honour their bravery."

The head-teacher wanted Mo, Monkey, Penguin and Hippo to tell the entire school about what had happened at the Botanical Garden. She wanted everybody to know about their heroic act.

Ms Qin wasn't quite so sure. She made a suggestion. "Perhaps the boys could start with just telling the rest of their class? Then they can speak to the whole school." Ms Qin knew the boys too well. She wanted to know what they were going to say, before they said it to the whole school.

"Fine, that's decided then," the head-teacher agreed. "I'll come over to your class to see how they do."

Ms Qin decided to let the boys tell their story to the class that very afternoon.

Mo said they would need to use the blackboard so that they could explain fully what happened, with diagrams.

Mo went up to the blackboard and started drawing. Hippo, Monkey and Penguin went up and helped out too.

First, Mo wrote down a title in really big letters using red chalk:

Honouring the Little Heroes

"Bravo! Bravo!" Hippo started clapping and then drew lots of thumbs-ups in different colours; Monkey drew lots of brightly coloured balloons, and Penguin drew lots of little cakes with cherries on them.

With all the thumbs-ups, balloons and cakes, the classroom suddenly had a carnival atmosphere.

As the bell rang, Ms Qin, the head-teacher and her deputy walked into the classroom. Ms Qin frowned when she saw what was written on the blackboard. Ms Qin thought the term "Little Heroes" wasn't very appropriate. She whispered to Man-Man and asked her who had written the words on the board. Man-Man said Mo had written them. Ms Qin was a little annoyed, but the head-teacher smiled and didn't seem to mind.

It was time to ask the Little Heroes to tell the class about their heroic act.

Ms Qin asked the four boys to stand in front of the class.

The four boys pretended to be very serious, but the other children started laughing. So the boys went back to being their normal playful and mischievous selves.

"All right, please begin! Who's going to speak first?" Ms Qin asked.

"Me! Me!" Monkey stood up to speak, but Mo quickly pulled him back to his seat.

"I saw the thief first! So I'm going to speak first!"

"But it was *me* who called the security guards!"

"The thief tied *me* up to a tree! Try and beat that!"

Mo and Monkey carried on arguing. Finally, Ms Qin decided that she would pick who should speak first.

"Since Mo saw the thief first, Mo, you can go ahead and speak first. How did you find out about the thief stealing the plant?"

Mo threw Monkey a victorious smile and began telling the story. "On the day of the Botanical Garden trip, I brought a rucksack with me. The bag was full of all kinds of tasty food, like fruit jellies, potato crisps—"

"Mo!" Ms Qin interrupted. "Get to the point!"

"OK, I will get to the point now," Mo scratched his head. "Where was I?"

Everybody laughed, even the head-teacher and her deputy.

Ms Qin asked Mo to sit down and think about what he was going to say.

"I'm next! I'm next!"

Seeing how desperately Monkey wanted to speak, Ms Qin gave Monkey the green light.

"As soon as I saw Mo being tied up by the thief, I quickly thought of a plan to save him. I went to find someone who could save Mo—"

Hippo and Penguin objected to this. "It was *us* who saved Mo, and *then* you went to call the security guards."

The class again burst out laughing.

Monkey was too embarrassed to go on, so Ms Qin asked Penguin to speak next.

Penguin said, "I am brilliant at the shotput! I was once ranked number six in the entire school—"

"Wrong! I was ranked number six, you were ranked number seven!" Hippo argued.

Everybody was confused. What did this have to do with stopping a thief?

"The man who tried to steal the fragrant thoroughwort hid on the other side of the wall. We picked an ideal spot and had our weapons ready."

"Our weapons were rocks," Mo added.

"As soon as the man poked his head above the wall, Mo ordered us to fire. Hippo and I threw our rocks at him as if they were grenades. My rock hit the man in the chest, and Hippo hit him on the shoulder. The man moaned in pain and fell down."

"Wrong!" Hippo argued. "It was my rock that hit the man in the chest; *your* rock hit him in the shoulder."

Ms Qin was glad it was only her class the boys were presenting their story to. Thank goodness she hadn't agreed to let the boys do it in front of the whole school. They wouldn't be able to stop squabbling. The head-teacher suggested that she should tell the whole school of the boys' heroic act, at the next assembly.

Meanwhile, before the day was over, Ms Qin spoke quite sharply to the boys about what had happened in the classroom. She said they may have been little heroes in the Botanical Garden, but they also needed to think about being little heroes in the classroom in the future. And that was that!

READER'S NOTE

MO'S WORLD

Mo Shen Ma lives in a big city in China. Modern Chinese cities are very much like ours, so his life is not so different from your own: he goes to school, watches television and gets up to mischief – just like children all over the world!

There are *some* differences, though. Chinese writing is completely unlike our own. There is no alphabet, and words are not made up of letters – instead, each word is represented by a little drawing called a *character*. For us, learning to read is easy. There are only twenty-six letters that make up all our words! But in Chinese, every word has its own character. Even Simplified Chinese writing uses a core of 6,800 different characters. Each character has to be learned by heart, which means that it takes many years for a Chinese school student to learn to read fluently.

NAMES

Chinese personal names carry various meanings and the names in this book have definitely been chosen for a reason! Take Mo Shen, the hero of our tale. His name is made up of the word *Mo*, which means "good ideas" and *Shen*, which means "deep" or "profound". So you can see how much his name suits him, because Mo Shen is always coming up with great ideas!

As usual, the other characters have also been given names that reflect their characters. Penguin's real name is Fei, which means "flying". This suits a boy who can rise into the air simply by holding in his farts! Monkey's real name is Chao, which means "above everyone". Very fitting for such a big fibber! And Hippo's real name is Da, which means "doing well". A perfect name for the always confident Hippo...

STORY BACKGROUND

Mo Shen Ma and his friends save several tubs of fragrant thoroughwort from a thief at the Botanical Garden. This herb – its Latin name is *Eupatorium Fortunei* – grows on grassy slopes and river beds in China and Japan. It is a small perennial bush with variegated green-grey leaves and pinkish white flowers which bloom in summer. It is very valuable in China because of its various medical uses: its leaves contain chemicals that can kill bacteria and viruses, prevent indigestion and bring down fevers! The leaves and stems are harvested in the summer, before the flower buds open, then dried for future use – usually brewed in a tea.

The plant is also considered beneficial for the circulation, and as such is often give to women who have just given birth. Finally, it is often ground into a paste and applied to the scalp in order to prevent dandruff. Perhaps the thief had a particularly bad case!